Diamond Life

BASEBALL

SIGHTS,

SOUNDS,

AND

SWINGS

CHARLES R. SMITH JR.

ORCHARD BOOKS ▪ An Imprint of Scholastic Inc. ▪ New York

I Remember . . .

I REMEMBER my first glove.

I REMEMBER sitting on my glove for hours to break it in.

I REMEMBER playing catch with my dad in the hot sun.

I REMEMBER watching my dad hit Wiffle balls into the bright blue sky.

I REMEMBER when the tree was first base, the pothole was second, the car was third, and the jacket was home base.

I REMEMBER hearing the *ping* of the bat on my first hit.

I REMEMBER scraping up the left side of my leg when I learned to slide.

I REMEMBER getting hit in the chest with a ground ball.

I REMEMBER being sent to the outfield because I couldn't field.

I REMEMBER learning how to block the sun with my glove to catch fly balls.

I REMEMBER catching my first fly ball.

I REMEMBER dropping many fly balls.

I REMEMBER striking out.

I REMEMBER my first home run.

I REMEMBER breaking my neighbor's window.

I REMEMBER playing rock, paper, scissors to figure out who would hop the neighbors fence to get the ball.

I REMEMBER bringing my glove to Dodgers games.

I REMEMBER my dad teaching me what all the positions were.

I REMEMBER eating hot dog after hot dog after hot dog after hot dog until I was sick.

I REMEMBER waiting to get my foul ball signed by the players.

I REMEMBER learning how to play "pickle."

I REMEMBER spitting contests.

I REMEMBER learning to hit from both sides of the plate.

I REMEMBER getting caught trying to steal home.

I REMEMBER my dad saying "good eye" whenever I drew a walk.

I REMEMBER when my dad could no longer play catch.

There are things I always forget, but when it comes to baseball, there are always things that I REMEMBER.

4

THAT SOUND?!

Pop!

Scratch

Whiff!

Whack!

Whoooooosh!

Zoom!

Spit

Crack!

Scratch

Smack!

Bloop

Slap!

Zing!

Scoop

Ping!

Clap!

B-I-N-G-O!

Come on, Billy, whaddya say, Bill-ay?! Let's get a **bingo**, Bill-ay. Billy, get a **bingo**! Get a **bingo**, Bill-ay! Atta boy, Bill-ay! Good eye, Billy! Way to take that ball, Billy. Way to take that ball. You wait for your pitch, Billy. Ya hear me? Wait for your pitch. Ohhhhhhhh . . . good cut, Bill-ay . . . good cut. Way to take a cut at that strike, Bill-ay.

Come on fellas . . . let's clap it up for Billy. Let's hear some chatter. Talk it up fellas, talk it up!

That's the way, Bill-ay. That's a good eye, Billy. Way to take that ball, way to take that ball, Billy! Wait for your pitch, Billy. You hear me, Billy boy? Wait for your pitch. Oh . . . oh . . . oh . . . !! Foul ball?!! That was a good cut there, Billy. Good cut! Come on, let's knock on some wood, Billy. Come on, Billy, I wanna hear you knocking on that wood, Billy. We need a **bingo** from ya, Bill-ay. **B-I-N-G-O**, Billy. That's what we need, Billy, is a **bingo**. A **bingo**, Bill-ay, come on, Billy-Billy, we need a **bingo**. GOOD EYE, BILLY!! Way to take that ball! Three and two, Billy boy. Full count, Billy boy. Way to hang in there, Billy, way to stay alive, Bill-ay! Wait for your pitch, Billy . . . wait for your pitch, Billy boy. Pitcher's got nothin' on you, Billy, nothin' on you, Bill-ay!! You got him, Billy boy . . . you got him. Now let's show him and get a **bingo**, Billy. Come on, Bill-ay . . . whaddya say, Billy boy . . . are we gonna see a **bingo**, Billy?

Come on, fellas, keep up that chatter for Billy boy. Let's get it goin'!

Billy goat's gonna get us a **bingo**, right, Bill-ay?! We need a **bingo** from ya, Bill-ay!! **B-I-N-G-O**, **B-I-N-G-O**, **B-I-N-G** . . . OH NO! Strike three?! That's ok, Billy. You did your best, Billy boy, you gave it your best shot. Way to hang in there, Billy goat, way to hang in there!

DIAMON

From behind the mask

my eyes do see

the game unfold

in front of me.

Around the horn

to first base I go

and witness the runner

stepping off slow.

Stepping and waiting

and hoping to steal

second base as

he digs in his heel.

To second

I slide

my eyes

and then fall

on the shortstop

pounding his glove

for the ball.

D VISION

Pounding

and punching

and shaking his mitt,

hoping to snatch

and steal a base hit.

As the outfielders wait

the third baseman debates

whether he should move in

or away from home plate.

Pawing and clawing

the dirt like a cat,

preparing to pounce

at the crack of the bat.

Back to the mound

I squint to see

the pitcher waiting

to throw strike three.

From infield to outfield

my eyes see it all,

while trying to focus

on catching the ball.

WHAT'S MY NAME?

They call me

The Dominator

Mound Intimidator,

Missile Throwing

High and Tight

Strike Activator,

Plate Painting Pinpoint Precision Locator.

Opponent Regulator

K Accumulator

Fireball-flinging Flame-throwing Fascinator

hurlin'

The High-heater

Across the Letters Streaker

Zippin' Hundred-Mile-An-Hour

Big Bat Swingin' Beaters

like

The Four-Seamer

The Super-Split-Finger

The Here-it-Comes-Hurry-Up-and-Wait Slow-Creeper,

The Midnight Rider

The Air-Slicing Slider,

The Five-Finger Knuckleball

Dust-kicking Glider . . .

. . . It's been a real pleasure
meeting you from the mound,
but now you have to go
'cause strike three means sit down.

13

"Man, did you see how far he hit that ball?! He almost got it over the center field fence," the young, freckle-faced ballplayer said.

"Ahh, that's nothing! You should've seen the homer I hit the other day that DID clear the fence. It put a dent in the scoreboard over there," another kid popped between bubblegum bubbles and silly smiles.

"A dent in the scoreboard, huh? That's not too bad for a rook. But listen, I once hit a ball so hard it cleared the fence AND the trees behind it," said another kid wearing his baseball cap backward and swinging a couple of bats.

"The trees . . . that's it? Listen kid, I once hit a ball so far that not only did I clear the fence AND the trees, the ball hit a telephone pole and put a hole in it. That's right, a hole. About the size of a fist. My fist . . . see! You can't even see the pole from here, that's how far it is," offered an older player furiously punching the center of his catcher's mitt.

"A hole in a telephone pole? I don't know about that. But I do know that I once hit a ball so hard and so high that it just kept going up and up and up and up and up and by the time it finally came down, it was all wet from dropping through rain clouds," a husky-voiced ballplayer added as he stood on the steps, staring at the sky.

"You guys are just talking loud and saying nothing! I once hit a ball so hard that it not only went past the fence, past the trees, AND past the pole, it sailed past your ball dropping through the rain clouds and said, " 'Look at me, I'm going to the moon! I'm going to the moon!'" a voice boomed from high atop a mountain of chiseled chest and shoulders.

TO THE

MOON

Bottom of the sixth. Down by one. Gotta get to second. Gotta get a run. *Gotta go. Gotta go.* Pitcher looks over. Not yet. Wait. Memorize motion. Anticipate. Watch. Right leg back. Glove up. Left leg kick up. Hesitate. Right arm back. Left leg plant. Release. *Strike.* Smooth motion. But slow. I got this guy. Leg goes up. Then fly. Fast. He's checking for me. Throws. Dive back. *Safe.* Again. That was close. Dust off pants. Fix helmet. Check gloves. Kick base. *Spit.* Catcher is eyeing me. Watch. Wait. Can he catch me? Let's see. Right foot off bag. Now left. Right foot dig. *Dig. Dig. Dig* up dust. Gloves touch dirt. Deep breath. Exhale. Here he goes. Watch. Wait. Anticipate. Right leg back. Glove up. Leg up. Hesitate. Go! Go! Go! *Faster. Faster. Faster.* Catcher catches ball. Stands. Fires. Feet first slide. Left leg out. Right leg under. Thighs kiss dirt. Ouch! *Slide. Slide. Slide.* Toes touch bag. Throw is too high. Too slow. Second base stolen. Dust off pants. Fix helmet. Check gloves. Spit. Two more to go.

"Listen,

Keep your eye on the ball.

Swing for the fences.

No matter how many times you strike out, keep swingin'.

The game ain't over 'til it's over.

Don't let the game control you; you control the game.

kid . . ."

Hit 'em where they ain't.

Slow down.

Hard work plus confidence equals success.

Practice patience.

Focus on what's in front of you.

Hey **batta-batta-batta-batta-battaaaaaa**! Whaddya say there **batta**? Let's see what you got **batta**! Show me something **batta**. Put me to work. Show me what you got **batta**. My feet are falling asleep out here. My glove's itching for something to catch. I got daisies sproutin' around my cleats I been out here so long!

Whaddya say **batta**? You gonna give me something to catch? Huh? You gonna send me a nice juicy fly ball so I can showcase my skills with this here big glove of mine? You gonna do that for me **batta**? You gonna give me something to chase so I can show off my speed?

Come on **batta**! Are you gonna send one up into the sky and make me blind my eyes? Are you gonna do that **batta**? Are you gonna make me use my sunglasses? You gonna make me use my sunglasses to rob you **batta**?

WAITING GAME

Whatcha-gonna-do **batta**? Huh? Whatcha gonna do? You gonna make me show off my backhand shoestring catch? You gonna do that for me? Huh **batta**? Do that for me **batta**. Put me to work!

Whaddya say? Put me to work **batta**! Get my cleats moving! Get my arm throwing! Send me over to the foul line so I can catch one of your foul balls! Send me crashing into the wall! Send me diving into the grass! Put some grass stains on my uniform for me **batta**!!

You gonna do that for me? Huh **batta**? You gonna put me to work or not? Come on **batta**, swing something my way. I wanna play, too!

Ball leaves hand.

Hand goes down.

Fingers spin.

Ball twirls 'round

and 'round

and 'round

and 'round

through the air.

THERE IT GOES!!

Ball reaches bat

CRACK!!

Is it fair?

Ball rises high

high to the sky.

It's going . . .

. . . it's going . . .

it's gone . . .

BYE-BYE!!!

There's nothing I hate more in the world than bad luck. Hate it. Can't stand it. Now I'm not talking about black cats, walking under ladders, or Friday the thirteenth, or anything like that. No. Things that happen during a baseball game that can give you bad luck. Things that if you do them can give you bad luck, or things that if you don't do them can give you bad luck. Know what I mean?

Let me explain. Everybody has their own routine when it comes to game day. Me . . . I'm no different.

For starters, one thing I don't do is touch the chalk lines on the diamond. Never touch the chalk lines on the field. Never. Never ever. Might be bad luck. Lots of things can give you bad luck when you're a pitcher. Especially when you're a pitcher. That's why I got these rules. Rules that I swear by so I don't catch any bad luck. Bad karma. Bad vibes. Bad voodoo, if you know what I mean. Some of the fellas say I'm too . . . what's that word . . . superstitious? But they don't know what I know when it comes to bad luck.

Take for instance this one time. I had a no-hitter going all the way into the eighth inning. Nobody could touch me. It was like the plate was three miles wide and I could throw the ball wherever I wanted and it'd be a strike. Nobody was hittin' me. Nobody. That is until the eighth inning when I took to the field and tripped over a patch of grass that made my right shoe kick up some chalk dust. And wouldn't you know that the moment it happened I knew, I just KNEW I was doomed. So what happens? A leadoff walk, a single, and a home run! BAM BAM BAM!! Just like that. From zero to three runs in the blink of an eye. Goodbye no-hitter. Hello bad luck.

That's why I came up with these rules. Rules that help me keep the bad luck away. I got so many of 'em I don't know where to begin. I don't want to bore you, so I'll just tell you a few.

RULE #1: Never touch the chalk lines on the field with your cleats. It's okay if the ball rolls on the line and you have to pick it up during a play, but never ever touch it otherwise. Oh yeah . . . I already told you that one.

RULE #2: Same meal before every game. Mac and cheese, two chili dogs, and a sour pickle (cut in half), washed down with an orange soda. The fellas think it's an odd combination. Maybe it is. It was the only thing we had in the house one day before a game and wouldn't you know it . . . I threw a shutout. So, every game day it's the same. Mac and cheese. Two chili dogs. Sour pickle . . . cut in half. Orange soda. I haven't thrown shutouts every game, but I haven't lost since then either. (Maybe it has something to do with the stomachache it gives me during the game. Haven't quite figured that out yet . . .)

Anyway . . . Rule #3 . . . Rule #3 . . . what is Rule #3? The socks? Oh yeah . . . **RULE #3:** Game socks don't get washed until I lose again. The same day I ate the mac and cheese and stuff was also the last day my socks got washed. I haven't lost since, so I don't know if it was the food or the socks. I figured I'd better not wash them just to be safe. My mom won't let me take my socks off in the car after a game so she gave me a mason jar to keep 'em in until the season is over. I used to keep it in my room but now I keep it in the garage because the flies like buzzing around it. I don't know why. Maybe they think the socks are lucky too.

RULE #4: Dusting the mound. I gotta gotta gotta always dust off the mound the same way every time before I throw a pitch. First I take my left foot and dig in behind the rubber. I dig in there real good so's to have a good spot to plant my foot. Then I take my right foot and kick the dust off the front of the rubber. Gotta do that before every pitch because you never know which batter could be bringing bad luck to the plate with him. So I kick the dust off the front as if I'm kicking the bad luck away. 'Cause that's what you gotta do. You gotta kick that bad luck away. Otherwise it'll kick you. That bad luck can really knock you out if you let it. Are you payin' attention to what I'm sayin'?

Anyway . . . where was I? Oh yeah . . . so RULE #5 . . .

Hop

skip

L

G

step   I hop

leap,   E   O   I step

I do   I skip

whatever   A   R   get hurt.

I can   so I don't

to keep   P   F   and leapfrog my cleats

sliding spikes   in dirt,

from sliding into   dig digging

my shins and my knees   fleet feet digging

as I leap over two

up high

I jump to catch

the ball

then pump

a rocket to first

that sizzles into

the first baseman's glove

as I quickly turn-two.

Welcome back, folks. If you've just tuned in, we've got a dandy of a game going on right here. The Yellow Jackets are up 2 to 1 on the Larks in the bottom of the ninth, with one man on. The fate of this game and the Larks' winless season now rests squarely on the bat of second baseman Adrian Roberts, who steps up to the plate with two outs gone already.

Pitcher T. J. Alexander, the hard-throwing lefty of the Jackets, has been masterful, hurling seven scoreless innings until allowing a home run in the eighth to Larks catcher Calloway Jones. That one mistake has set up this moment, folks—Alexander the heat-hurler versus Roberts the big swinger.

Roberts steps up to the plate and makes himself at home in the right-side batter's box. Alexander struck him out on his last at bat, but Roberts seems to have shrugged that off. His eyes narrow in on Alexander as he awaits the first pitch. Alexander checks the runner on first and then goes into his windup. STRIKE ONE! The split-finger heater right down the pipe! Roberts was WAY behind on that one as Alexander nailed his spot.

The home crowd here is on their feet, anxiously waiting as Roberts kicks the dirt from his cleats and then settles back in for pitch number two. Alexander doesn't even look over to first base. He wants the batter in the box: Roberts.

Alexander goes into his windup. Roberts focuses. His gloves tighten their grip on the slim end of the bat and . . . STRIKE TWO! That sinker dropped right off the table from twelve to six o'clock. Roberts never had a chance.

Alexander receives the ball back from the catcher and wastes no time on the mound. He tugs his cap and toes the rubber with movements as crisp as the breeze snapping the "LET'S GO LARKS!" banners held by these anxious fans.

Roberts steps out. His eyes dart across the banners in the crowd and then he digs back in, furiously chicken scratching a hole in the batter's box. A jersey tug here. A sleeve pull there, and Roberts is ready. He sets his bat in motion, spinning minicircles with the bat head like a bee circling a hive. Will this bat bring the joy and jubilation of a win, or the sadness and despair of yet another loss? Only . . .

Alexander deals on the 0-2 pitch. A sidearm whip cracks a heater right down the pipe as Roberts . . . CONNECTS!! All eyes look to the sky. Will this Lark leave the park? It's high . . . it's fair . . . it's . . . it's . . . GONE!!! THE LARKS HAVE LEFT THE PARK!! THE LARKS HAVE LEFT THE PARK!! Ladies and gentlemen, Adrian Roberts just launched a moon shot that still hasn't landed to win the game for the Larks! There is cheering in the stands! There is dancing on the field! There is joy! There is celebration! All because there is a WIN, brought to you with one MIGHTY swing of the bat!!

"I didn't catch the ball because the sun was in my eyes."

"I t^{ri}pp_ed over a gopher hole and dropped the ball."

"I didn't strike out, I just didn't see a pitch I liked."

"This bat is too heavy."

"This bat is too small."

"The catcher smells so bad that he made me strike out."

"The second baseman tripped me."

"My glove is too **big**."

"My glove is too small."

"I meant to throw the ball into the stands."

"I didn't drop the ball, I let the ground catch it."

"I was standing in the field so long that my feet fell asleep."

"I dropped the ball because the pitcher spit on it."

"I meant to run into the wall and drop the ball."

"I let the ball go between my legs so the outfield could get it."

BASEBALL AND ME

When I was growing up in Los Angeles, California, my father frequently took me to Dodgers games. I remember eating lots of foot-long hot dogs (famous at Dodger Stadium), going onto the field before the game to have the players sign my ball, and getting free treats on the special days, such as "hat day," "bat day," or "towel day."

But what stands out most are the shared moments between me and my dad—the two of us just watching a game and having a good time. Those moments were made all the better by my father teaching me the basics of how to play. How to stand in the batter's box. How to catch a fly ball. How to throw a fastball. I wanted to be a pitcher, and he caught as many balls as I could hurl at him until he couldn't squat anymore.

Those moments with my father also taught me that baseball is a sport with lots of quirks. Like the rituals and superstitions some players had, or specific words that were used in the game itself.

In creating this book, I wanted to show my love for the game through photographs and words that were inspired by my memories of watching and playing the game as a kid. Now that I'm a father, I've taken my own kids to a few minor league games and have started tossing a ball around with each of them. My son tells me he wants to be "the one that throws the ball a lot."

"You mean, a pitcher?" I ask him. (Looks like I'll be doing lots of squatting soon.)

"Yeah, a picture. That's what I want to be," he says and then hurls a Wiffle ball at me with his left hand. (Left-handed pitchers are always in demand.)

I look forward to taking him and his sister to their first Yankees game. I can't wait to see their reaction to that moment when the crowd is still, and then all of a sudden . . . **SMACK** . . . it's going . . . it's going . . . **IT'S GONE! AND THE CROWD GOES WILD!!!**

—CHARLES R. SMITH JR.